THE FUTURE IS BRIGHT

Ellyn Sanna
with Viola Ruelke Gommer

BARBOUR
PUBLISHING, INC.

You've reached the end of
all that yesterday held—
and now you're standing
on the edge of tomorrow.
Everything the future holds
is waiting for you,
like a stack of gifts ready for you to open.

As you step into tomorrow,
rely on God's guidance and love.
The future He has planned for you
is glorious and bright!

THE FUTURE IS BRIGHT

As you move into your future,
I pray that you will. . .

* Hold On to Your Dreams
* Never Let Obstacles Stand in Your Way
* Rely on God's Promises
* Build Strong Now. . .for the Future
* Believe That the Best Is Yet to Come

In the past we have had a light which flickered,
in the present we have a light which flames,
and in the future there will be a light
which shines over all the land and sea.

WINSTON CHURCHILL

. . .

THERE IS ALWAYS ONE MOMENT. . .
WHEN THE DOOR OPENS
AND LETS THE FUTURE IN.

GRAHAM GREENE

ONE

HOLD ON TO YOUR DREAMS

The dream comes through much effort. . . .

ECCLESIASTES 5:3 NASB

AS YOU FACE THE FUTURE,
I KNOW YOU ARE FILLED WITH DREAMS.
DON'T LET THOSE DREAMS SLIP AWAY.
SOME DAYS YOU WILL BE DISCOURAGED.
SOME DAYS YOUR DREAMS WILL
SEEM LIKE IMPOSSIBILITIES.
BUT HOLD TIGHT TO YOUR DREAMS.
MAKE THE EFFORT.
ONE DAY, YOU'LL LOOK AROUND—
AND REALIZE THAT THE REALITY
GOD HAS CREATED
IS FAR BETTER THAN
EVEN YOUR WILDEST DREAMS.

The Future is Bright

Now that you're an adult, you'll find you have both new freedoms and new responsibilities. Don't let either rob you of your dreams. No matter how busy you are, no matter how many new interests fill your hours, you'll find that the simplest things of life are full of the deepest meaning and beauty. Don't become blind to those simple things; don't lose your childhood ability to dream.

Because it's in our dreams where we often touch Eternity.

. . .

Life is so full of meaning and purpose, so full of beauty,
beneath its covering that you will find that earth
but cloaks your heaven.

Fra Giovanni

Inevitably, sooner or later, you'll run into people who will doubt your ability to follow your dreams. "It can't be done," they'll tell you. "You have to be practical."

Don't listen to their voices. Remember: I believe in you. And so does God.

. . .

THOSE WHO BELIEVE IN OUR ABILITY
DO MORE THAN STIMULATE US.
THEY CREATE FOR US AN ATMOSPHERE
IN WHICH IT BECOMES EASIER
TO SUCCEED.

JOHN LANCASTER SPALDING

THE FUTURE IS BRIGHT

WE ALL NEED DREAMS TO LEAD US INTO THE
FUTURE. THOSE DREAMS GIVE US VISION—
AND VISION BEGINS IN THE HEART. . . .

. . .

Be brave enough to live life creatively. The creative is the place where
no one else has ever been. You have to leave the city of your comfort
and go into the wilderness of your intuition. You can't get there by
bus, only by hard work and risk and by not quite knowing what you're
doing. What you'll discover will be wonderful. What you'll discover
will be yourself.

ALAN ALDA,
advice to his daughter

THE FUTURE IS BRIGHT

As you face the future, what may hold you back is not so much the pressures of reality. . .

as the surrender of your dreams.

No one can force you to make that surrender, however. . .

so hold on to your dreams. Take time to dream new dreams.

God has no limits!

Be patient. With God's mighty power, your dreams can be birthed into reality.

. . .

Live deep instead of fast.

HENRY SEIDEL CANBY

The Future is Bright

If your determination is fixed, I do not counsel you to despair.
Few things are impossible to diligence and skill.
Great works are performed not by strength, but by perseverance.

Samuel Johnson

. . .

To accomplish great things, we must dream as well as act.

Anatole France

. . .

Despise not small things, either for evil or good,
for a look may work thy ruin, or a word create thy wealth.
A spark is a little thing, yet it may kindle the world.

Martin Farquhar Tupper

You're going to be busy in the years to come.
New relationships, new opportunities,
new responsibilities will claim your
attention. And those are all good things.
But don't allow yourself to be distracted.
Look straight ahead,
follow your dreams,
listen to your heart,
and reach high for your goals.
Together, you and God
can create an amazing future.

TWO

NEVER LET OBSTACLES STAND IN YOUR WAY

We can say with confidence,
"The Lord is my helper,
so I will not be afraid.
What can mere mortals do to me?"

HEBREWS 13:6 NLT

You are beginning a new venture
on your journey through life.
The course ahead will not always be
smooth—but it will be exciting,
filled with wonder and achievement.
Don't allow obstacles to slow you down. . .
Instead, evaluate each day. . .
Learn from the challenges you face. . .
Take each day's lesson with you. . .
And leave the rest behind.

The Future is Bright

Celebrate the accomplishment
and satisfaction of each day. . .
no matter how small. . .
Appreciate the new gifts each day offers. . .
And then move on. . .
Always ready for more lessons. . .
more accomplishments.
Enjoy the journey!

So let us know,
let us press on to know the Lord.
His going forth is as certain as the dawn;
and He will come to us like the rain,
like the spring rain watering the earth.

Hosea 6:3 NASB

THE FUTURE IS BRIGHT

I don't mean to say that I have already achieved these things
or that I have already reached perfection!
But I keep working toward that day when I will finally be all
that Christ Jesus saved me for and wants me to be. No. . .
I am still not all I should be, but I am focusing all my energies
on this one thing. . .looking forward to what lies ahead,
I strain to reach the end of the race and receive the prize. . . .

PHILIPPIANS 3:12–14 NLT

. . .

It is not a question of. . .what we bring with us,
but of what God puts into us.

OSWALD CHAMBERS

"Don't be afraid! . . . For there are more on our side than on theirs."

2 KINGS 6:16 NLT

. . .

A MAN MUST NOT DENY HIS MANIFEST ABILITY, FOR THAT IS TO EVADE HIS OBLIGATIONS.

ROBERT LOUIS STEVENSON

. . .

Great ability develops and reveals itself increasingly
with every new assignment.

BALTASAR GRACIÁN

THE FUTURE IS BRIGHT

DON'T BE AFRAID OF THE OBSTACLES YOU FACE.
THEY MAY EVEN OFFER YOU NEW OPPORTUNITIES.
IN THE MIDST OF THE OBSTACLES,
YOU WILL FIND NEW AND UNSUSPECTED PATHS.
THESE PATHS WILL LEAD YOU TO SUCCESS
YOU NEVER THOUGHT TO IMAGINE.
HAVE COURAGE. . .
GOD'S BLESSINGS ARE WAITING FOR YOU.

The Future is Bright

Do not let what you cannot do interfere with what you can do.

John Wooden

. . .

Obstacles are those frightful things you see when you take your eyes off your goals.

Unknown

. . .

If you think you can or can't, you're always right.

Henry Ford

THREE

RELY ON GOD'S PROMISES

The fulfillment of God's promise depends entirely on trusting God and his way, and then simply embracing him and what he does. God's promise arrives as pure gift.

ROMANS 4:16 THE MESSAGE

THE FUTURE IS BRIGHT

IN THE BIBLE,
YOU WILL FIND MANY PROMISES FROM GOD.
THESE PROMISES ARE LIKE STEADY
STEPPING-STONES THAT WILL LEAD YOU FORWARD
INTO THE BRIGHT FUTURE
WHERE GOD WANTS YOU TO LIVE.
BECOME FAMILIAR WITH THESE PROMISES—
AND CLAIM THEM AS YOUR OWN. . . .

The Future is Bright

Surely goodness and love will follow me all the days of my life,
and I will dwell in the house of the LORD forever.

PSALM 23:6 NIV

· · ·

No eye has seen, nor ear heard, nor the human heart conceived, what God has prepared for those who love him.

1 CORINTHIANS 2:9 NRSV

· · ·

Our God gives you everything you need,
makes you everything you're to be.

2 THESSALONIANS 1:2 THE MESSAGE

THE FUTURE IS BRIGHT

Your heavenly Father knows your needs.
He will always give you all you need from day to day.

LUKE 12:30–31 TLB

. . .

THE LORD SAVES THE GODLY;
HE IS THEIR FORTRESS IN TIMES OF TROUBLE.
THE LORD HELPS THEM,
RESCUING THEM FROM THE WICKED.
HE SAVES THEM,
AND THEY FIND SHELTER IN HIM.

PSALM 37:39–40 NLT

. . .

The LORD is a shelter for the oppressed,
a refuge in times of trouble.

PSALM 9:9 NLT

THE FUTURE IS BRIGHT

SEEK YOUR HAPPINESS IN THE LORD,
AND HE WILL GIVE YOU YOUR HEART'S DESIRE.
GIVE YOURSELF TO THE LORD; TRUST IN HIM,
AND HE WILL HELP YOU;
HE WILL MAKE YOUR RIGHTEOUSNESS SHINE
LIKE THE NOONDAY SUN.
BE PATIENT AND WAIT FOR THE LORD TO ACT;
DON'T BE WORRIED ABOUT THOSE WHO PROSPER
OR THOSE WHO SUCCEED IN THEIR EVIL PLANS.
DON'T GIVE IN TO WORRY OR ANGER;
IT ONLY LEADS TO TROUBLE.
THOSE WHO TRUST IN THE LORD
WILL POSSESS THE LAND. . . .
THE LORD GUIDES. . .AND PROTECTS
THOSE WHO PLEASE HIM.
IF THEY FALL, THEY WILL NOT STAY DOWN,
BECAUSE THE LORD WILL HELP THEM UP.

PSALM 37:4–9, 23–24 TEV

THE FUTURE IS BRIGHT

GOD'S PLANS FOR YOUR FUTURE INCLUDE. . .

Exploration,
Meaning,
Discovery,
Fulfillment,
and Purpose.

TRUST HIM TO GUIDE YOU IN THE DAYS AHEAD.
RELY ON HIS PROMISES.

FOUR

BUILD STRONG NOW. . .FOR THE FUTURE

*I am about to do a new thing;
now it springs forth, do you not perceive it?*

ISAIAH 43:19 NRSV

You may feel as though the future
you long for is still beyond your reach.
There is more you have to do before it
arrives—and some days it seems so far away.

But the future doesn't magically appear out
of thin air. Whether or not you realize it,
right now you are creating the future.
The way you live your life today. . .and
tomorrow. . .will influence the shape
of your life for years to come.

THE FUTURE IS BRIGHT

GOD NEVER GIVES STRENGTH FOR TOMORROW
OR FOR THE NEXT HOUR,
BUT ONLY FOR THE STRAIN OF THE MINUTE.

OSWALD CHAMBERS

. . .

The future is purchased at the price of vision in the present.

SAMUEL JOHNSON

The Future is Bright

We should all be concerned with the future because we will have to spend the rest of our lives there.

Charles Franklin Kettering

. . .

Enjoy present pleasures in such a way as not to injure future ones.

Seneca

. . .

None of us knows what lies ahead. . . . The important thing is to use today wisely and well, and face tomorrow eagerly and cheerfully and with the certainty that we shall be equal to what it brings.

Channing Pollock

THE FUTURE IS BRIGHT

The future enters into us, in order to transform itself in us,
long before it happens.

RAINER MARIA RILKE

. . .

LIGHT TOMORROW WITH TODAY!

ELIZABETH BARRETT BROWNING

. . .

Enough, if something from our hands have power
To live, and act, and serve the future hour.

WILLIAM WORDSWORTH

Each day you are building the house
in which you will live for the rest
of your life—and for eternity.
So lay a firm foundation for your house.
Put in lots of windows.
Make sure the door is strong
enough to withstand life's storms—
and opens easily to let in
new experiences and people.
Create a haven that will last a lifetime.
Don't forget to make room for guests—
especially God's Spirit.
Build strong.

FIVE

BELIEVE THAT THE BEST IS YET TO COME

"No eye has seen, no ear has heard,
and no mind has imagined
what God has prepared
for those who love him."

1 CORINTHIANS 2:9 NLT

YOU'LL HEAR PEOPLE TALK ABOUT
THE "GOOD OLD DAYS."
AS YOU LEAVE YOUR CHILDHOOD BEHIND,
YOU MAY BE TEMPTED TO DO THE SAME.
SOMETIMES, THE PAST LOOKS SO MUCH ROSIER
THAN THE PRESENT OR FUTURE.
BUT THAT'S MERELY AN ILLUSION.
TRUE, EACH PHASE OF YOUR LIFE
WILL HAVE ITS CHALLENGES—
BUT EACH PHASE WILL ALSO HAVE JOYS YOU
COULD NEVER HAVE IMAGINED AHEAD OF TIME.
GOD HAS GREAT THINGS PLANNED
FOR YOUR FUTURE. TRUST IN HIM.
THE BEST IS YET TO COME.

THE FUTURE IS BRIGHT

There are better things ahead than any we leave behind.

C. S. LEWIS

. . .

LEND ME THE STONE STRENGTH OF THE PAST
AND I WILL LEND YOU
THE WINGS OF THE FUTURE, FOR I HAVE THEM.

ROBINSON JEFFERS

. . .

You can never plan the future by the past.

EDMUND BURKE

The Future is Bright

Begin the new day before you by. . .

> * Living up to the best in yourself;
> * Keeping faith with the past;
> * Caring, loving, and sharing.

God will guide and strengthen you as you face each day's new light.
He has wonderful things in store for you.

THE FUTURE IS BRIGHT

Learn from the past. . .but don't allow it to draw the boundary lines for your future. Just because things have always been a certain way, doesn't mean they will always be that way in the future. God loves to surprise us. And His only boundary lines are love.

. . .

The Lord says, "Do not cling to events of the past
or dwell on what happened long ago.
Watch for the new thing I am going to do."

ISAIAH 43:18–19 TEV

THE FUTURE IS BRIGHT

AS YOU FACE A FUTURE BRIGHT WITH GOD'S LOVE, MAY THIS BE YOUR PRAYER:

I'm asking God for one thing, only one thing:
To live with him in his house my whole life long.
I'll contemplate his beauty; I'll study at his feet.
That's the only quiet, secure place in a noisy world.

PSALM 27:4–5 THE MESSAGE